APRIL SHOWERS

By **George Shannon**

Pictures by
Jose Aruego and Ariane Dewey

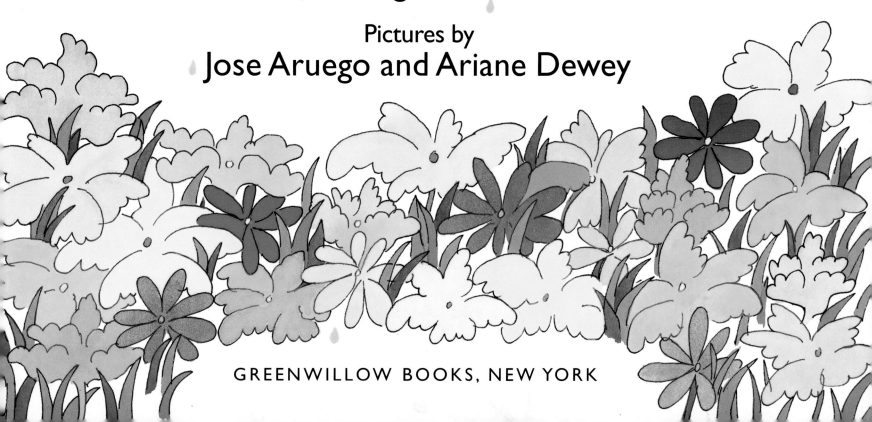

GREENWILLOW BOOKS, NEW YORK

Library of Congress Cataloging-in-Publication Data
Shannon, George.
April showers / by George Shannon ; pictures by Jose Aruego and Ariane Dewey.
    p.   cm.
Summary: A group of frogs enjoys dancing in the rain so much that they seem
not to notice a snake sneaking up on them.
ISBN 0-688-13121-2 (trade).   ISBN 0-688-13122-0 (lib. bdg.)
[1. Frogs—Fiction.   2. Snakes—Fiction.   3. Dancing—Fiction.]
I. Aruego, Jose, ill.   II. Dewey, Ariane, ill.   III. Title.
PZ7.S5287Ap   1995   [E]—dc20   94-6266   CIP   AC

FOR SUSAN VALENTINE—
who invited me into the wonderful rain
— G. S.

FOR JUAN
— J. A. and A. D.

When the clouds roll in and the rain comes down,
The frogs in the garden hop around and shout:
"Ladies and gentlemen. Children, too.
"We've just GOT to do a dance for you.

"We're gonna tip-toe twirl.
We're gonna twirl, toe tip!
We're gonna grab hands, kick, circle round for you.
We're gonna step-back-hop.
We're gonna hop-turn-slide.
We're gonna momma-step, papa-step, scissor-step, too.

"We do what's right.
We play by the rules.
But when the rain comes, we love to dance like fools!

"We're gonna—Oops!—flutter-kick.
We're gonna kick-turn-spin.
We're gonna step, double-skip, leap high, split, too.
We're gonna slow-step-spin.
We're gonna spin-quick-kick.
We're gonna shimmy shimmy shimmy, spin-kick for you.

"We do what's right.
We play by the rules.
But when the rain comes, we love to dance like fools!

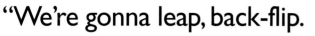

"We're gonna leap, back-flip.
We're gonna flip right back.
We're gonna tap triple-splat, spin-splash for you.
We're gonna tap-turn-twist.
We're gonna twist and shout!
We're gonna skip, boogie woogie—No, you don't!—jump, too.

"We do what's right.
   We play by the rules.
   But when the rain comes, we love to dance like fools!

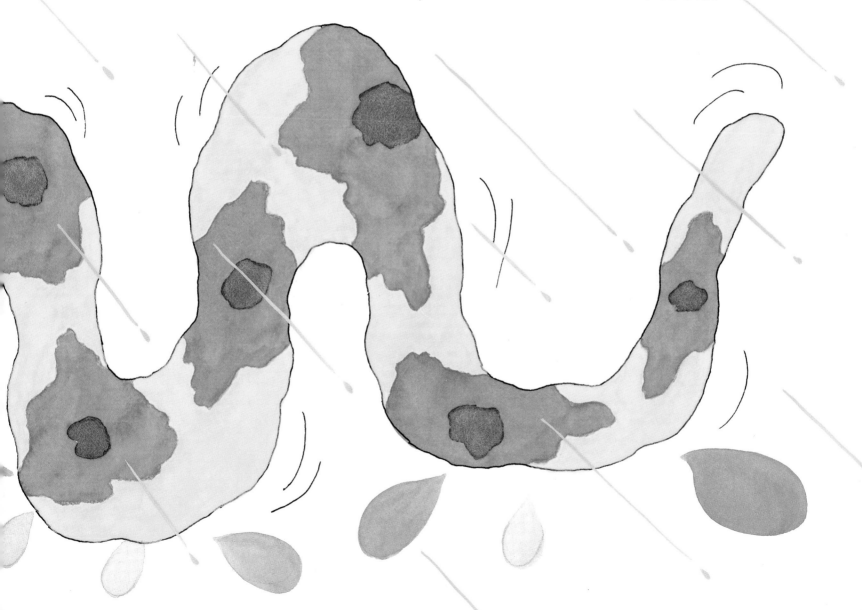

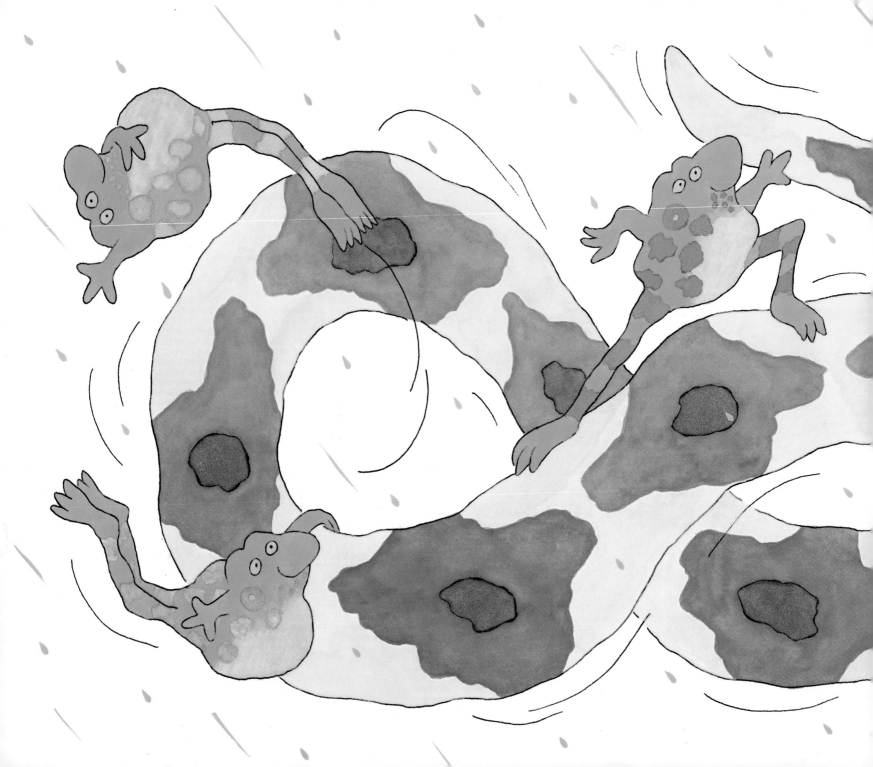

"We're gonna spin-jump-splash.
We're gonna splash-tap-spin.
We're gonna twirl, somersault, twist-flip for you!

"We do what's right.
We play by the rules.
And when we get to dancing, we're nobody's fools.

"Oh, when we get to dancing, we're NOBODY'S fools.
We just danced our favorite tale for you!"

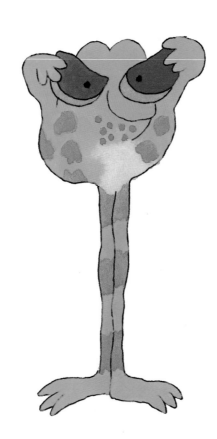